Mariella Mystery

Investigates

The Disappearing Dinner Lady

Look out for more books about
Mariella Mystery

The Ghostly Guinea Pig
A Cupcake Conundrum
The Huge Hair Scare
The Curse of the Pampered Poodle
The Spaghetti Yeti
A Kitty Calamity

Mariella Mystery
Investigates
The Disappearing Dinner Lady

by Kate Pankhurst

Orion
Children's Books

First published in Great Britain in 2015

by Orion Children's Books
an imprint of Hachette Children's Books
a division of Hodder and Stoughton Ltd

Carmelite House
50 Victoria Embankment
London EC4Y 0DZ
An Hachette UK Company

1 3 5 7 9 10 8 6 4 2

The paper and board used in this paperback are natural and
recyclable products made from wood grown in sustainable forests.
The manufacturing processes conform to the environmental
regulations of the country of origin.

A catalogue record for this book is available from the British Library.

ISBN 978 1 4440 1234 7

Printed and bound in Great Britain
by Clays Ltd, St Ives plc

www.orionchildrensbooks.com

For my school dinner buddies –
Fi, Jen and Nic

BE STEALTH, LIKE A SHADOW!

CLUES! CLUES Clues

hat

Me, wearing my badge.

ROBO DoG

Woof! Woof! Beep!

SUPER POWERED SNIFFER CIRCUITS

THIS YOUNG SUPER SLEUTH JOURNAL BELONGS TO ...

Mariella Mystery, that's me! Totally amazing girl detective, aged nine and a bit.

I'm so good at solving mysteries, I think it's about time I won an award – that's why I've awarded myself an Official Mega-Mystery-Girl Badge of Honour.

(NOTE: If you are thinking of making another attempt to steal my badge, Arthur, don't bother. There's no way I'll slip up and leave it on my jumper in the washing basket again.)

BADGE

MEGA Mystery GIRL

THE PUDDLEFORD PRIMARY PRESENTS...

Princess and the Pea

Parents are invited to the performance in the school hall,

Friday 22nd May 12PM

Is she a real princess? The only way to find out is to see if she gets a wink of sleep lying on a pea plucked from the vegetable patch at Puddleford Primary.

STARRING PRIMROSE PARRINSON

PEA

WARNING: Contains silly songs about peas and lots of dancing. (Not how proper detectives spend their time, but there was no getting out of it.)

PICK me!

Sunday 17th May

Mariella

v olet

POPPY

NOTE: Mum has finished knitting our runner bean costumes (she runs an online knitting shop called Knitted Fancies (You Name It, We'll Knit it.) Even though these look quite silly, we might need them if a mystery involving vegetable theft occurs.

wool

3:30PM
MYSTERY GIRL HQ
(TREEHOUSE IN MY GARDEN)

This afternoon's incident shows that I can't afford to let my Mystery Senses tune out, not even for a moment.

CASE REPORT: OPERATION REALISTIC RUNNER BEAN UPDATE

1:30PM: Poppy has made us rehearse our entrance on-stage seven times - tiptoeing across HQ and finishing with a little heel kick and hand wave. (Apparently if a runner bean came to life, it would totally act like this.)

tip toe

heel kick

Poppy Holmes: Mystery girl with amazing acting talents. We don't have any lines in the play, so Poppy says we should dedicate our time to becoming Masters of Disguise. She said if we can be realistic runner beans, we can pretend to be anything.

POPPY with a runner bean

Violet on the mystery beanbag.

Violet Maple: Totally cool Mystery Girl. Pleased me and Poppy can support her through her stage fright. (I've told her she has nothing to be worried about because we've been in mystery situations far more dramatic than a play about a pea.)

I'm alive!

Mariella Mystery

(me): Mystery is what I do, that's why I'm a Mystery Girl. Master-of-Disguise training might be useful in the future, but I'd prefer a real and dramatic mystery to solve.

me, at the mystery desk.

1:45PM: Poppy tells me and Violet to carry on practising while she goes to the loo or we'll never be convincing runner beans, just three girls jumping around in green tights.

1:47PM: Poppy bursts back into HQ, performing a new move. Me and Violet try to follow but we can't keep up. Poppy runs around in circles, waving her hands and knocking things over. This definitely doesn't seem like something a runner bean would do.

1:55PM: I tell Poppy to slow down. Poppy ignores me, grabs our hands and makes us spin in a circle.

1:59PM: Violet screams for it to stop and we land in heap on the floor, but Poppy's legs are a blur of green tights as she kicks them wildly in the air.

2:00PM: I shout at Poppy that there's no way we'll ever remember all these moves.

2:01PM: The door to HQ swings open. Poppy appears. She stares at us, shocked.

POPPY?

2:02PM: I have a terrible realisation. The runner bean lying next to me, still kicking its legs in the air as if it is being electrocuted, is not Poppy. How did I not notice this runner bean was shorter than the real Poppy? The Mystery Girls have been tricked and I know exactly who by!

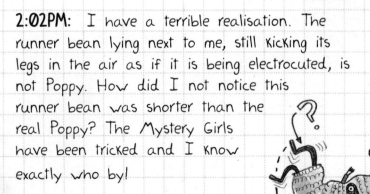

IMPOSTER RUNNER BEAN: Arthur Mystery. Totally annoying younger brother. He has been cast as a roast potato, but due to his ridiculous phobia of potatoes, he is desperate to switch roles.

Arthur doing an annoying dance →

2:10PM: Arthur is finally ejected from HQ and Poppy says this is a huge setback in our practice schedule because she needs to leave early to buy some new green tights. (Arthur has put a hole in hers.)

hole

2:11PM: I say this is a huge setback in our detective careers. I didn't immediately detect a false Mystery Girl - there is clearly something very wrong with my Mystery Senses.

2:12PM: The rest of the Move Like a Runner Bean practice session is officially cancelled.

Spaghetti Bolognese

5:25PM
MY HOUSE, 22 SYCAMORE AVENUE
(DINNER TIME, SPAGHETTI BOLOGNESE)

Mum and Dad aren't taking what Arthur did seriously at all. Mum says Arthur is feeling uncertain about being a potato in the play and it's making him have emotional outbursts. She says I should be more understanding because I know why he has a phobia of potatoes.
Ugh. How could I forget?

Ever since Arthur had an allergic reaction after eating a potato flavoured Monster Mash Meal-in-a-Mug* soup, he's refused to eat anything containing potato.

itch!
itch!
ARTHUR'S RASH

15

*MEAL AND PUD-IN-A-MUG:

Instant soup and pudding range launched by celebrity children's TV chef, Arabella

Flump, two years ago. Arthur, along with loads of other kids, loved them so much that supermarkets struggled to keep up with demand. Unlike Arthur, I had important detective work to do, so couldn't just sit around after school slurping Meal-in-a-Mug like he did.

I had a lucky escape though, because it was revealed that the Meal and Pud-in-a-Mugs caused terrible allergic reactions. Symptoms included a weird rash, uncontrollable trumping and throwing up. Kids all over the country got sick. The products were instantly banned and Arabella Flump was officially forbidden from working as a chef ever again.

Arthur goes on and on about how overcoming the itchy illness means that he is totally brave enough to become a Mystery Girl. I don't think so. Let's look at the evidence:

EVIDENCE ARTHUR IS NOT CAPABLE OF EVER BEING A MYSTERY GIRL:

A: Arthur is scared of potatoes. Small, round, non-terrifying vegetables.

↑ potatoes

wimp

B: He is afraid of the roast potato costume he has to wear in the school play. It's a pillowcase.

C: He is not a girl and we aren't changing the name of our detective agency to the Mystery Girls and a Boy.

I have been so annoyed I totally forgot I have the perfect revenge to use against Arthur!

The other day I was looking for an empty cereal box to make a new fake beard, and I found a leftover multipack of Meal and Pud-in-a-Mugs! Mum

concealed Meal and Pud-in-a-mug!

thought she'd thrown them all away, but they were sitting right at the back of the cupboard. I can't wait to see Arthur's face when I tell him they have been touching his Chocco Flakes box for months now. Ha!

I'm not going to mention it now, though, not while Mum and Dad are making a final decision about whether I can swap from packed lunches to the amazing new school dinners. Violet and Poppy's parents have already agreed, but that's no good unless I can too. We can't discuss cases if I'm on the Packed Lunch Table and they are on the Hot Dinners Table.

7:15PM

MY BEDROOM, 22 SYCAMORE AVENUE. MYSTERY DESK

At last! Mum and Dad delivered their decision and it's a YES! I'm so pleased I can just about get over the fact Arthur is switching too. He wants to do everything I do, which is highly annoying.

I rang Poppy and Violet to tell them the good news. We tried school dinners once before, but that was when The Big G was in charge, and they were disgusting.

Vegetable mush

THE BIG G (AKA MISS GLENDA BUTTON):

Head Dinner Lady at Puddleford Primary. (Known as the Big G because she has a BIG voice that she uses to shout at people who refuse to eat her disgusting speciality dish - Vegetable Mush.)

THE BIG G ♪ Glenda Button

The Big G and four other dinner ladies have been off sick for three weeks now, because there has been an outbreak of Dinner Lady's Finger.*

*DINNER LADY'S FINGER: An illness commonly suffered by dinner ladies, because they have damp hands from washing up. The infection spreads from the hands, causing uncontrollable itchiness and flaky skin all over the body that might drop into school dinners. Eurgh! Mum said she knew a dinner lady who had it once and it was far worse even than when Arthur had his allergic reaction.

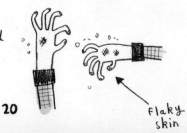

flaky skin

Some new dinner ladies have arrived, from Ladies Who Lunch Supply Dinner Lady Agency – and they can cook!

DIANA DUMPLING: Star Dinner Lady, working for Ladies Who Lunch. We already knew Diana because while she was at college studying the Dinner Lady Code of Conduct, she worked in the newsagent on Poppy's street. She said it was her dream to be as successful at dinner-ladying as her mum and grandma, who are both dinner ladies and have published books about school dinner recipes. (The Big G needs to read one.)

Diana Dumpling

Contains loads of RULES

THE DINNER LADY CODE of CONDUCT

It was an amazing surprise when Diana turned up three weeks ago. Every lunchtime, while she clears tables, we've been having in-depth discussions about mysteries we've solved. (She's totally not just pretending to be interested, like other grown-ups do.)

Everyone is going crazy for a dessert* invented by Diana. It's why the Mystery Girls definitely wanted to swap to hot dinners. I cannot wait to try it tomorrow!

*MONDAY MUNCHIE MADNESS: A chocolate pudding served on Mondays, which contains hidden

monday munchie Madness

healthy ingredients. So it's chocolate and good for you! Roberta Poppet in Year Four let Violet try some of hers last week. Violet said it tastes like a cloud of chocolate melting in your mouth - she knows stuff about baking and apparently a fluffy chocolate cake like that is really hard to achieve.

MONDAY
18th May

Saffron
Cauliflower

NOTE: Ladies Who Lunch normally refers to ladies who go out for lunch all the time, but in this case refers to dinner ladies who come to schools and whip up delicious lunches! It's run by Head Dinner Lady, Saffron Cauliflower. (Much friendlier than the Big G.)

Pick a Pea dance

1. Pick a pea. 2. Pick me. 3. I never liked the garden anyway.

10:40AM
PUDDLEFORD PRIMARY GIRLS' TOILETS, MORNING BREAK

I'm glad it's breaktime, because now it isn't too long until we try Diana's pudding, and also we can have a rest from singing the rubbish song about the Queen picking a pea from our school's vegetable patch. (Our class has just finished a rehearsal for *The Princess and the Pea*.)

> **'Pick a Pea, Pick me!
> I never liked the garden anyway!'**

As we were leaving the hall, Diana came out of the kitchen. We told her the great news that we'd see her in the queue at lunch for some of her famous pudding.

"I'll look forward to it!" said Diana, smiling.

"I was wondering actually," Violet added, "if I could get your chocolate pudding recipe? I'd love to be able to make cake as fluffy as you do."

yum!

Violet

"Oh, sure," said Diana. "I'll be busy at lunchtime, but I've got to call into the supermarket later. Meet me there? About four o' clock?"

"Great!" said Violet, grinning at me and Poppy.

Cool! Most teachers and grown-ups pretend they haven't seen you outside of school, like Miss Twist did at Puddleford Cinema last week, but Diana actually wants to meet us. I know it's to give Violet a recipe, but I'm sure it's also because she knows we are totally professional mystery-solvers who have loads of interesting stuff to say.

12:20PM
LUNCHTIME, PUDDLEFORD PRIMARY HALL

What we've just witnessed was totally weird.

Everyone was going back to class while the
dinner ladies set up the hall for lunch, so I
suggested to Miss Crumble that me, Poppy and
Violet stay behind to hang up the vegetable
costumes. What I really wanted to do was make
sure we were first in the school dinner queue. It
was a good job Miss Crumble agreed, or we'd
have missed the whole thing.

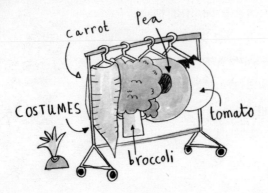

carrot

Pea

COSTUMES

tomato

broccoli

CASE REPORT

mrs Potter

mrs Price

mr Douglas

11:52AM: Costumes are sorted. The dinner ladies and man don't look up from setting out the tables as we walk across the hall.

11:53AM: As we approach the closed serving hatch, a loud and distressed-sounding scream comes from the kitchen.

ARGHHHHEEEEEEEEEEEEE!

11:54AM: The dinner ladies and man don't seem to have heard the scream over the noise of tables being dragged, but my Mystery Senses leap into action. Somebody is in need of Mystery Girl assistance!

11:55AM: We race towards the kitchen, through the door marked 'Staff Only'. Has Diana's pudding exploded everywhere? Is Saffron Cauliflower trapped under a massive tin of baked beans?

11:56AM: The kitchen looks normal. Silver trays of tasty school dinners are lined up by the serving hatch. Saffron Cauliflower walks out of the storeroom. Spotting us, she looks puzzled. We ask if everything is OK because we heard a scream of terror.

PUZZLED

11:57AM: Saffron laughs. She says the dishwasher in our school is the most ancient thing she's ever seen. It makes a screaming noise when steam escapes from it. She also says it's nice that we were on high alert, but we aren't supposed to be in the kitchen.

11:58AM: Violet and Poppy laugh too, and turn to leave. I feel silly, but I notice that we didn't see Diana setting up tables outside and she isn't in the kitchen. I ask where she is.

11:59AM: Saffron is distracted trying to open the serving hatch. She says, "Miss Dumpling? Oh, she doesn't work for Ladies Who Lunch any more." Me, Poppy and Violet are all thinking the same thing. WHAT?

12:00PM: The serving hatch slides open, revealing a huge queue. I quickly ask Saffron why Diana left her dream job. Saffron says not to worry because there will still be a delicious pudding today.

12:01PM: I want to ask more questions, but the other dinner ladies have come in now. Mrs Price tells us get out, though not as nicely as Saffron.

NEW MYSTERY TO SOLVE: WHAT HAS HAPPENED TO DIANA DUMPLING? THE DISAPPEARING DINNER LADY.

(Violet says that Diana hasn't actually disappeared, she's just stopped working here. But it's a catchy title for this mysterious revelation.)

SIGNS OF MYSTERY: ACTING OUT OF CHARACTER

If somebody you know well begins to act in a manner that is unusual for them (acting out of character), it could be a sign that a mystery situation is unfolding. Can you distinguish between someone who is having a bad day, someone in need of your help – or someone who might, in fact, be a master criminal?

Spotting The Signs:

BECOMING WITHDRAWN: Investigate further if a bubbly person you know seems quieter than normal. Are they being blackmailed about a terrible secret from their past?

Alone

EXCESSIVE TWITCHINESS: Is this person restless because of a guilty conscience? Check news reports for details of terrible crimes. Ask yourself, how well do you know this person?

Twitchy

ACTING IN A ZOMBIE-LIKE MANNER: Sometimes, villainous criminals hypnotise innocent individuals and force them to do their dirty work (jewellery theft, catnapping etc).

← In a trance

IGNORING PHONE CALLS: This may mean that a friend finds you boring. Although, as you are an exciting Young Super Sleuth this is unlikely. Could they have been kidnapped?

Ring, ring
Ring, ring

OVERENTHUSIASTIC LAUGHING: Is this person genuinely amused? Or are they trying to cover up a guilty conscience? Why not track this person's movements to make sure?

Verging on hysterical

WARNING

I know your secret!

We all have days when we don't feel ourselves. If you accuse somebody of being up to no good when, in fact, they just had a bad night's sleep — you may end up with few friends.

YAWN!

31

12:35PM
DINNER HALL, PUDDLEFORD PRIMARY

Diana Dumpling isn't the only thing to disappear.
Her famous pudding has too.

It didn't take long for news to ripple down the
lunch queue that Monday Munchie Madness had
been replaced with Princess Pie* dessert and that
Diana was nowhere to be seen.

PRINCESS PIE: Massive pink
jelly with green frog prince-
shaped sweets and jelly
crowns inside. Impressive
but not impressive enough
to distract us from
what has just
happened.

Princess
Pie

sweets

Saffron told kids who asked what was going on the same thing she'd told us – Diana doesn't work for Ladies Who Lunch any more, but that it doesn't mean an end to tasty puddings.

This is so weird. Diana acted like everything was fine when we saw her at break.

"Shouldn't Saffron be more bothered that her star dinner lady is gone? She doesn't even look a bit upset," I said. "And what does 'she doesn't work here any more' even mean? That Diana resigned? Or … could she mean Diana was sacked?"

"What?! Diana would never do something to get herself sacked!" Violet said.

"But, Violet, it doesn't make any sense that she'd choose to leave her dream job either," Poppy said.

"Well, I'm sure Diana will explain everything when we meet her," Violet replied.

Hmmm. Maybe. But would Diana definitely still meet us later – if her day had suddenly gone so badly wrong? We needed to explore all the logical explanations:

Logical (But Unbelievable) Explanation One:

Diana did something really bad – like cutting her toenails in the kitchens. Saffron

ha ha!

was forced to sack her and Diana screamed. Saffron made up the story about the dishwasher and is pretending not to seem shocked because she doesn't want anyone to find out the terrible truth about Diana.

But Diana has studied the Dinner Lady Code of Conduct so she wouldn't suddenly forget dinner lady rules about spreading germs, would she?

toenail germs

Logical (Possible) Explanation Two:

After break, Diana found out she'd won a Best Dinner Lady in the Whole World competition and has been whisked away to write a school dinner cookery book. The scream we heard was Diana with delight. Saffron made up the story about the dishwasher because she is jealous of Diana's success.

Wouldn't Diana have said if she'd entered a Best Dinner Lady in the World competition? Also, that scream didn't sound like a happy scream - it was definitely more of a terrified ARGH! Spider in the bath! sort of scream.

Spider

(Sort Of) Logical Explanation Three:

Diana realised that she was the best Dinner Lady in the World and decided to leave and set up her own rival dinner lady agency. The scream we heard was Saffron because she couldn't believe Diana would do such a thing.

fuming

But Diana was really happy to get a job at Ladies Who Lunch - would she really want to leave and set up her own company so soon?

VERDICT: We have decided to question Saffron further - she must know what happened and we're not totally sure she was telling the truth about the scream. The dinner ladies usually go home when they've finished tidying up after lunch, but Saffron does Head Dinner Lady stuff and is sometimes still around until the end of school.

dishwasher

ARRGHEEE!

2:20PM
PUDDLEFORD PRIMARY SCHOOL HALL,
AFTERNOON BREAK

We located Saffron at the start of break, as she was leaving the kitchens. I explained we are actually detectives, so she should just tell us why Diana doesn't work here any more.

"I've been serving lunch to proper detectives? Wow!" Saffron said. "However, it would go against the Dinner Lady Code of Conduct to discuss the personal matters of my staff. I do have a real mystery you could solve for me though – why is it so hard to get lumps out of custard?"
She winked and strode off.

Saffron being secretive

Hmm. Maybe there were rules Saffron had to follow or maybe she was hiding something. But just because she doesn't want to talk, doesn't mean we should give up. (Also, we are capable of solving far more complicated mysteries than why custard is lumpy.)

"Emergency kitchen search needed!" I said.

"I'm not sure about this. We aren't supposed to go in there. Is it really worth getting into trouble when we'll probably see Diana later?" said Violet.

Violet (worried, as usual.)

Until we know for sure the reason Diana left, I think a possible scream and a missing star dinner lady *is* worth getting into trouble for. If we don't search the kitchen now, clues could be tidied away and missed forever. I'm going in and I don't care what Violet says, she and Poppy are coming too.

2:40PM
PUDDLEFORD PRIMARY, MISS CRUMBLE'S CLASSROOM

The kitchen was empty. Silver worktops and fridge fronts sparkled. My eyes darted around, looking for the ancient dishwasher Saffron had mentioned.

kitchen

empty

I think Poppy was letting the drama of the search get to her. She dashed over to the bin in the corner, put on a pair of gloves from the Mystery Kit and started shoving rubbish covered in slimy school dinner goo into evidence bags.

evidence?

"What?" she said, when I gave her a funny look. "There might be something in here that proves Diana broke a rule. The Young Super Sleuth's Handbook says Bin Sifting is an excellent way to turn up clues that have been disposed of."

I wasn't sure any of the soggy stuff Poppy was pulling out was going to be useful, but there wasn't time to argue. Saffron could come back at any moment.

I spotted the dishwasher in the far corner, next to the storeroom. I'd been expecting to find some sort of really rusty old machine, but it looked the same as everything else in the kitchen. Sparkling and new. Weird.

sparkling

"Look at this!" Violet shouted, from the other side of the kitchen, by the dinner ladies' pigeon holes.* She was waving a slip of paper.

Pigeon

coo coo.

*PIGEON HOLE: Doesn't actually contain pigeons, it's a compartment with a person's name on for putting letters and paperwork in.

I raced over, thinking it might be Diana's resignation letter, explaining why she had quit. Then my tummy did a back-flip because the unbelievable might be true, and what if it was an official letter about her being sacked?

"It's Diana's recipe for Munchie Madness Chocolate Pudding!" Violet said.

I was a bit disappointed. Finding a recipe wasn't going to tell us anything important. Then I spotted something written at the bottom:

Monday Munchie
Pudding Recipe

2 cups flour
3 eggs
3 spoonfuls of honey
Cocoa powder

HEALTHY HIDDEN VEGETABLES

2 cups grated carrot
1 cup grated beetroot
1/2 cup grated courgette

Mystery Girls, things are not what they seem.

"Erm. What does that mean?" said Poppy.

"It must mean the pudding, of course. Chocolate pudding is usually unhealthy, but this one is full of vegetables." Violet shrugged.

I'm not sure. I've read loads of stuff in the Young Super Sleuth's Handbook about detectives ignoring clues because they thought they weren't relevant.

"It might mean that, but so far today we've heard a scream that hasn't been properly explained, found out that Diana suddenly doesn't work here any more, and discovered a cryptic message addressed to the Mystery Girls," I said. "Something definitely isn't right."

"Maybe Diana was planning to give us this note after school, but she had to leave in a rush and forgot it," Poppy said, looking excited.

"I'm sure Diana will be able to clear up this whole misunderstanding when we meet her," Violet said.

I hope so. I'd usually be really excited about a mystery situation like this – I just wish it wasn't Diana who was involved.

Diana's house

5:45PM
23 PEARTREE AVENUE, DIANA DUMPLING'S GARDEN WALL

We waited outside the supermarket for over half an hour, but Diana didn't show up.

If the reason she left Ladies Who Lunch was for something nice, like winning a competition, I'm sure she would have tried to get a message to us. Not showing up suggests something bad happened and she's too upset to meet us.

us. Waiting

"Diana is probably fine and just forgot about our meeting because it's been a hectic day," Violet said. "Like the time I forgot we had a Mystery Meeting because I found out I'd been picked to look after the class hamster."

Chip (hamster)

I hope Violet is right. Whatever has happened, we at least want to know Diana is OK – especially if it was her we heard scream. (The dishwasher did NOT look ancient to me.)

Poppy remembered the name of Diana's street, so we decided to come here and see if we could find her. We knocked on a few doors and one of her neighbours told us which house it was. She isn't home, so we've been waiting outside for a bit in case we spot her on her way back.

We've been here for ages now and I suppose there isn't much point in just sitting on Diana's garden wall with no idea of when she is due home.

I should probably
put the Mystery
Kit in the wash too.
The evidence in the
bags Poppy collected
from the kitchen bin
earlier is, as I suspected,
just loads of empty food
packets and – GROSS ALERT –

one of the bags has leaked school dinner goo all
over the Mystery Kit. Poppy!

Before we left, I remembered some advice from
The Young Super Sleuth's Handbook about taking
logical steps to find out the truth.

"Let's leave Diana a note asking her to get in
touch," I suggested.

My mystery notepad was soggy so I had to use
a page from Violet's Kitten Cuddles Weekly
Planner. It didn't really look like something a
serious investigator would use, but Violet said
Diana likes kittens and it might cheer her up if
she is in distress.

This is what we wrote:

The Mystery Girls
22 Sycamore Ave

Hi Diana,

We called round to check you are
OK. We were TOTALLY shocked when
Saffron told us you didn't work
at school anymore.

As you know, The Mystery Girls
are trained detectives, so if
you need our help, or if things
are 'not what they seem' then
get in touch.

Love Mariella, Poppy and
Violet
xxx

PS: Does the dishwasher at
school scream? You might
think we are crazy but we
are checking it wasn't you
who screamed because you need
our help.

kitten cuddles

NOTE: Diana hasn't contacted us, yet. I asked Dad if there had been any report at the Puddleford Gazette (where he works) about a dinner lady winning an amazing prize. So far, nothing, Dad says he'll let us know if there is.

Tuesday 19th May

Diana—looking distraught

10:40AM
PUDDLEFORD PRIMARY SCHOOL
PLAYGROUND, MORNING BREAK

Before break, our class was rehearsing in the hall again. This was good because it meant we could keep an eye on the kitchen and listen for clues, like one of the dinner ladies saying really loudly, "I can't believe Diana left to set up her own dinner lady agency" or the dishwasher screaming, or something like that.

The stage

me

PICK ME

PRINCESS THE and the PEA!

Miss Crumble was getting us to practise our entrance when ...

ARGHHHHEEEEEEEEEEEEE!

The second suspicious scream coming from the kitchen in two days!

"It's the dishwasher! It does scream!" Violet said.

But that noise didn't sound much like steam escaping from a dishwasher to me – it sounded like a very annoyed person.

BANG!

The kitchen door slammed open and the Big G stormed into the hall. A flustered Miss Twist and Saffron Cauliflower followed.

I made an emergency deduction – the Big G had recovered from Dinner Lady's Finger sooner than anyone had thought and she was really angry about something.

"I DO NOT NEED COOKING LESSONS!" the Big G yelled. "ESPECIALLY NOT FROM THAT CAULIFLOWER WOMAN!"

I could see the other dinner ladies gawping from around the kitchen door. (The dinner ladies who had been off with Dinner Lady's Finger were back too.)

miss Twist

Saffron

"Miss Button, we do school dinners the Ladies Who Lunch way now," Miss Twist said. "If you don't like it, I'm sure Saffron is more than capable of running the kitchen."

I thought the Big G might be about to shout something else, but she must have taken Miss Twist's threat seriously because she folded her arms and huffed back into the kitchen.

That explains the scream – it definitely wasn't the dishwasher this time. So what happened yesterday? Operation Surveillance Sandwich* is officially launched.

*OPERATION SURVEILLANCE SANDWICH:

Lunchtime is the ideal opportunity to get closer to the dinner ladies (and man) to find out what they know about Diana's disappearance. The Mystery Girls will act like the pieces of bread in a sandwich, closing in on our tasty filling (dinner lady information).

surveillance
Sandwich

ARGH!
Vegetable
mush!

12:50PM
SCHOOL HALL, LUNCHTIME

NEW INFORMATION ALERT!

Here are the results of our lunchtime mission to observe and extract information from dinner ladies (and a dinner man):

OPERATION SURVEILLANCE SANDWICH:

12:10PM: Two new Ladies Who Lunch dinner ladies are serving lunch. They are called Mrs Spooner and Mrs Brewster. They tell us they have been drafted in to help teach new recipes to the Big G and her team.

mrs Spooner

mrs Brewster

12:11PM They are both really chatty - until I ask about Miss Dumpling. They glance at each other, then Mrs Brewster says very politely that we are holding up the queue.

12:12PM: The Big G flings spoonfuls of lunch onto our plates. She keeps giving Saffron Cauliflower dirty looks.

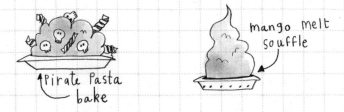

dirty look

dollop!

NOTE: (Cooking lessons appear to be working, Pirate Pasta Bake with skull and crossbone-shaped pasta and Mango Melt Soufflé are TASTY.)

↑Pirate Pasta bake

mango melt souffle

12:35PM: Saffron starts clearing the table next to us. I decide to use a cunning technique from the Young Super Sleuth's Handbook called Making Innocent Conversation to Draw Out Information.

my innocent face

12:36PM: I say that we have been looking into the Lumpy Custard Mystery and we should have some answers soon. Saffron is delighted. Now I have her attention I say we'd love to help, because she must be working extra hard getting the new dinner ladies used to our school kitchen now Miss Dumpling isn't around.

Lumpy Custard

12:37PM: Saffron beams and says it's sweet of us to worry, but everything is fine and that she meant what she said yesterday - Miss Dumpling leaving is absolutely nothing for us to fret about.

12:38PM: Before she walks off, Saffron notices we haven't finished our lunch and calls, "Come on, girls! That food won't finish itself. YUM, YUM! IN MY TUM!" (She's always saying that. It's embarrassing - we're not little kids!)

yum yum

12:40PM: Mr Douglas (dinner man) is sweeping the floor. As he goes past our table I say I can't believe what I've heard about Diana. (This is another Young Super Sleuth technique called Pretending You Know More Than You Do To Extract Information.)

12:41PM: Shaking his head, Mr Douglas says it's terrible that everyone knows and he couldn't believe it when Mrs Cauliflower told him she had to sack Diana for misconduct. Violet chokes on her pudding.

SHOCK REVELATION ALERT ONE: Our worst fears are true! Diana didn't choose to leave - she was sacked!

12:42PM: Mr Douglas says that Diana must have broken an important rule in the Dinner Lady Code of Conduct to be told to leave immediately. Then he says we are being really nosy, and that, actually, he probably shouldn't be talking to us about it.

12:42PM: I think quickly and ask if Mr Douglas has ever heard the dishwasher scream like a crazy person.

12:43PM: Mr Douglas raises an eyebrow. He makes a joke about screaming when he has to do the washing up. Then he says since the fancy new dishwasher was installed you can't even tell when it's on because it's so quiet.

SHOCK REVELATION ALERT TWO: Saffron made up a story about the dishwasher and we did hear someone scream yesterday!

VERDICT: The evidence suggests we have solved the mystery of what happened to the Disappearing Dinner Lady. She was sacked! And the scream we heard yesterday was almost definitely her. I had hoped this wouldn't be true, but now we have proof that it is, I can't get my head around it.

CASE CLOSED

guilty!

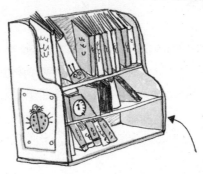

2:00PM
EMERGENCY MYSTERY GIRL MEETING, MISS CRUMBLE'S CLASSROOM, READING AREA

We are supposed to be having small group practice sessions for the play, but I can't focus. There are too many unanswered questions. Like, what is Diana supposed to have done? Why did Saffron lie about the scream? Have we really been completely wrong about Diana Dumpling? And what did she mean in her note by 'things are not what they seem'?

"I'm as shocked as you, but things *are* what they seem," Violet said. "Diana disappeared because she was sacked and whatever she did, she didn't want to tell us about it. Saffron fibbed because she was embarrassed that we heard Diana scream. End of mystery."

I know what Violet is saying – the mystery of why Diana disappeared does seem as if it's been solved – but what sort of detectives wouldn't want to get the full story? I want to (and not just because I can't quite believe Diana was sacked) because without the details, our final case report would just read: **'STAR DINNER LADY SACKED**. Who knows what terrible thing she was supposed to have done? We never bothered to find out.'

Our case file

"The case is solved but it's unfinished," I said. "We don't have all the facts. If we find out the truth, maybe there'll be a way of helping Diana get her job back."

"I don't know, Mariella. You've got a lot of faith in Diana. Not everyone is as amazing and reliable as me and Violet," said Poppy.

I couldn't believe Poppy and Violet were just going to accept they'd got Diana wrong. To me this felt as crazy as hearing your lovely, fluffy old granny was going to prison for a terrible and mysterious crime.

granny

"If I was sacked from being a Young Super Sleuth, would you two say, 'Oh dear, we must not have known Mariella very well – we won't even bother to find out what she is supposed to have done'?" I said. (The Young Super Sleuth's Handbook calls this having a highly persuasive argument.)

"Of course you wouldn't," I continued. "You'd get the full story, and that's what we need to do. If we find out Diana was sacked for something so awful there's no coming back from it, well, I'll just write that in our case report and accept that I can never trust my Mystery Senses again."

Being able to trust your Mystery Senses is probably the most important part of being a detective so it would be awful to find out mine have been wrong. I'm sure they're not. I totally would have picked up on it if Diana was a rule breaker.

EXhibit A: REBEL DIANA

SECRETLY WILD

grubby fingernails

muck

not following hair net proceedure

The Young Super Sleuth's Handbook says not to let the fact you like somebody get in the way of your judgement and I'm totally not doing that. At least, I don't think I am. I just want all the facts.

We are going to look for Saffron to tell her we know Diana was sacked and she may as well just tell us what for. We are also planning to visit Diana's house again and some of her other known hangouts.*

*KNOWN HANGOUTS: Places you know you are likely to spot a person you are looking for. In Diana's case, we know she often visits Puddleford Library, BAArmy (wool shop) and the newsagent at the end of Poppy's street where she used to work.

UPDATED MYSTERY STATUS: In DISGRACE!
the disappearing dinner lady is in disgrace - is she washed up or can she sparkle again?

5:45PM
MYSTERY GIRL HQ

As we were leaving school today, Poppy spotted something that made me think we are totally right to keep investigating.

We've taken this Ladies Who Lunch information leaflet off the parent's noticeboard in school reception.

SAUSAGE SURPRISE

CHEESY CHOMP PASTA

ALPHABETTI APETISER PIE

PRINCESS PIE

MANGO SOUFFLÉ

NUTZ ABOUT NOODLES

PIRATE PASTA BAKE

MUNCHE MADNESS CAKE

MEET DIANA DUMPLING, DINNER LADY IN CHARGE OF RECIPE DEVELOPMENT.

We already knew Diana was an amazing dinner lady, but none of us knew she'd invented all the Ladies Who Lunch recipes. I'm sure Diana would have been was really proud Saffron had given her such a big responsibility – especially when she hadn't been a dinner lady for very long. It makes it even more difficult to believe that Diana would have deliberately done anything to risk her job.

All we know for sure is that it's proving difficult to get the full story.

"I'd love to chat but things are busy, busy, busy!" Saffron said, when we tried to catch her at afternoon break.

Diana was nowhere to be seen at her likely hang-outs and when we went by her house again after school. I tried calling through the letterbox. There was no reply.

Either Diana was out or she was ignoring us. I have to admit, lying low like this does sort of suggest she has a guilty conscience. It's really frustrating.

How are we ever going to get any proper explanations with Diana hiding away and Saffron and all the other dinner ladies avoiding our questions?

Diana moping in her dressing gown

6:30PM
MY BEDROOM, 22 SYCAMORE AVENUE

We'd been trying to decide what to do for ages
when Poppy jumped off the beanbag she'd been
sitting on and waved the Ladies Who Lunch
parent information leaflet.

"Masters of Disguise training!" she shouted.

I couldn't believe she was suggesting that we
have a Move Like a Runner Bean Rehearsal
instead of figuring out this case. She didn't mean
that, though.

"The leaflet has an address on it for Ladies Who Lunch Head Office!" Poppy said. She was right. I hadn't noticed the small Puddleford address on the back cover.

"We could go there as undercover dinner ladies! There might be a clue to tell us why Diana was sacked," Poppy said. "You two are getting really good at being runner beans so you could definitely pretend to be dinner ladies."

Violet looked at Poppy as if she was crazy, but this was exactly the sort of genius detective thinking we needed!

"It'll never work – we are way too young to look like proper dinner ladies," Violet said.

"The Mystery Girls are Masters of Disguise," I said. "We can be whoever we want to be!"

It's all planned. Tomorrow
after school, we are
going to visit the Ladies
Who Lunch head office and
pretend to be new recruits.

Mavis   VERA

If we look like we work for Ladies Who
Lunch, somebody might totally spill the
beans about why Diana was sacked.

Pauline

Dinner ladies are much more likely to gossip
with other dinner ladies about what's going on.

Poppy said we could have a night off from
practising being a runner bean as long as we
promised to channel* our inner dinner lady.

*CHANNELLING: When you focus your mind
on becoming somebody else. I tried to channel
my inner dinner lady by wiping the table after
dinner. I must have been believable
because Mum said it was
like there was a totally
different person in
the room.

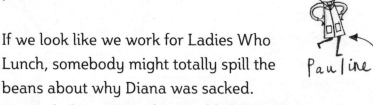

me. channelling
my inner dinner
lady.

DISGUISES: APPEARING OLDER THAN YOU ARE

A true Master of Disguise is able to transform themselves convincingly from an energetic Young Super Sleuth into a much older person. It only takes one childish slip up to blow your cover.

To Look Older You Will Need:

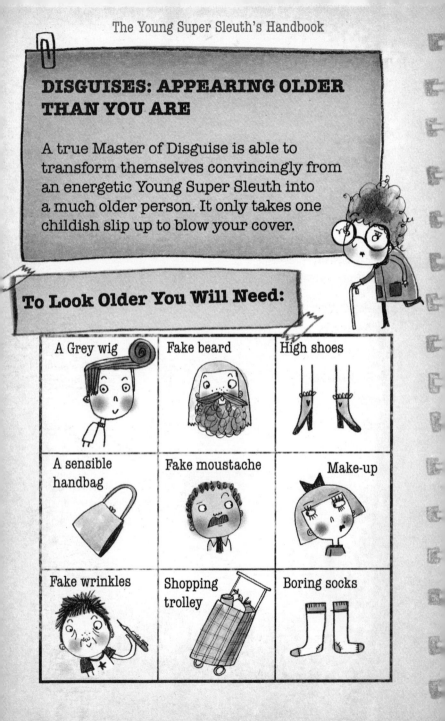

A Grey wig	Fake beard	High shoes
A sensible handbag	Fake moustache	Make-up
Fake wrinkles	Shopping trolley	Boring socks

To Sound Older, Try Saying the Following:

Ooooh. My back!

My memory isn't what it was.

Years and years and years ago, when I was young ...

Can you repeat that, please? I'm a bit deaf.

Honestly, I never have a moment to myself.

I don't like rollercoasters, they look so unsafe.

Stylish grown-up neckerchief →

Actually aged nine

TOP TIP

Less is more. Using all of these suggestions at the same time may make your disguise unconvincing.

DISGUISES FOR OPERATION
DINNER LADY DUPE*:

Lab coats

Platform shoes. To look taller

Hairnets.
(shower caps with lines drawn on.)

me, WEARING LIPSTICK

Lipstick.

DUPE*: Tricking somebody into thinking something, like that the Mystery Girls are actually dinner ladies.

Wednesday 20th May

NOTE: The Mystery Kit still needs to be washed. (I had to put it in a carrier bag by the washing machine because the smell was so disgusting.) We are using Poppy's monster rucksack as a temporary Mystery Kit.

Temporary mystery kit

LUNCH

Alphabetti Appetiser Pie

Strawberry Surprise pudding

12:30PM
PUDDLEFORD PRIMARY SCHOOL HALL,
LUNCHTIME

Poppy has been really distracted all morning.
She's heard there is a bug going around Year Six,
and that both the Princess and the Pea (and a
few other main parts) will need stand-ins if they
aren't better in time for Friday's performance.

She has been humming the Pick a Pea song all
morning, just in case she is asked to audition.
I keep reminding her we
need to focus on
our plan for
this afternoon
instead.

hum
hum
hum
HUM!

Violet thinks the Big G might have persuaded the Puddleford Primary dinner ladies and man to walk out in protest about the cooking lessons because it's lunchtime and none of them are here. Saffron Cauliflower has taken over on table wiping duty and the new Ladies Who Lunch dinner ladies, Mrs Spooner and Mrs Brewster are serving.

I'd be surprised if Mrs Potter, Mrs Price and Mr Douglas walked out because they didn't seem to mind working with Ladies Who Lunch. Perhaps they've all been sent for intensive cooking lessons somewhere?

A few minutes ago Miss Twist and Saffron were having a serious looking discussion by the water jug table, near to where we were sitting.

SERIOUS DISCUSSION

I thought it might be something to do with where the dinner ladies are, or maybe even what happened to Diana, so I tried to listen in. But all I heard was Miss Twist worrying about what school dinner canapés* to serve for parents on Friday.

*CANAPÉS: Small posh party food. Miss Twist wants to let all parents know how amazing our school dinners are now so she will be serving Tingling Tomato Vol-au-vents and Mini Pirate Pasta Bake Bites.

small

I might have heard something else useful to our enquiry if Poppy hadn't started chair dancing, trying to get Miss Twist to notice her acting talent. Miss Twist shouted at Poppy to act sensibly and walked off. Honestly. I hope she pulls herself together before our mission.

chair dancing

4:45PM
OUTSIDE THE SNAPPY SHOPPER
SUPERMARKET, CATCHING OUR BREATH

Our visit to Ladies Who Lunch revealed some
TOTALLY unexpected information.

CASE REPORT: OPERATION DINNER LADY DUPE

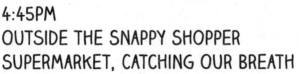

4:05PM: We locate the Ladies Who Lunch
Head Office above the Roll It
Out carpet shop. At
street level, there is a
red door with a small
gold 'Ladies Who
Lunch' sign on it.

ROLL IT OUT

Ladies Who
Lunch HQ

4:06PM: I press the intercom button. Poppy tells us to remember our Masters of Disguise training, but to definitely not get this mixed up with Thinking Like a Runner Bean, because that will blow our cover.

BUZZ

4:10PM: The receptionist picks up. Poppy says that we are the new recruit dinner ladies, here for training. There is a click. The door is open.

4:12PM: Sally (the receptionist) waits at the top of the stairs. I brace myself for her to tell us that we don't look like proper dinner ladies, but she just says that dinner lady training was yesterday and she wasn't expecting any more new recruits.

4:13PM: Poppy replies that we thought training was this afternoon. Then says it's a shame if we're wrong, because our friend, Diana Dumpling, said training was loads of fun. (Argh! Poppy was meant to wait until we'd gained people's trust before bringing Diana up!)

4:14PM: Sally's eyebrows almost fly off her forehead. (She clearly knows something about why Diana was sacked.)

Receptionist

4:16PM: The receptionist asks us to wait a moment and says that her boss, Mrs Cauliflower, is in her office and will know what is going on. She leaves the room and the click of her high heels fades away down the corridor. Oh no!

click

click

4:17PM: Violet is talking really fast about how Saffron will recognise us and we'll get in trouble and we should run. I tell her to breathe. We're not leaving without progressing to Phase Two of our plan. (PHASE TWO: If nobody will talk, conduct a search of the premises.)

4:18PM: We leap into action. Well, me and Poppy do. Violet listens at the door for approaching footsteps.

FEAR

79

4:20PM: I turn around to see that Poppy is shoving rubbish from the bin into the new monster Mystery Kit rucksack, just like she did in the school kitchen the other day.

4:21PM: I'm about to tell Poppy that an apple core is not evidence when she shouts that she has found something - it's Diana's Dinner Lady Employee File! Poppy shoves it in the Mystery Kit.

4:22PM: Violet squeaks that she can hear footsteps. We hear Saffron saying she definitely hasn't hired any other new dinner ladies. I close the cupboard door and give the codeword - runner bean! (This means make a run for it.)

4:23PM: We race down the stairs and escape to Puddleford High Street. I glimpse back and see Saffron in the doorway. She looks confused. Has she recognised us? We don't hang around to find out.

confused

OUTCOME: MISSION SUCCESSFUL.

EVIDENCE UNCOVERED:

EMPLOYEE FILE

NAME: Diana Dumpling

DISMISSED FOR SERIOUS MISCONDUCT*:
Infringement of Rule 344 of the Dinner Lady
Code of Conduct.

The conduct mentioned here wasn't the only
rule broken but this alone was so shocking
I was forced to skip an Official Warning and
dismiss Diana Dumpling with immediate
effect. By far the worst rule breach I have
ever seen in all my years of being a head
dinner lady.

Saffron Cauliflower

SERVICES
TERMINATED

LADIES WHO LUNCH SUPPLY DINNER LADY AGENCY

*SERIOUS MISCONDUCT: Misconduct is when
you do something that goes against all the rules
of your job, which for dinner ladies might be
causing food poisoning or stealing another dinner
lady's handbag.

SAFFRON CAULIFLOWER'S LUNCHBOX: Poppy grabbed it just in case it was important. It isn't. Contains an empty flask and some sandwich crusts.

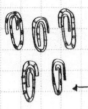

FIVE PAPER CLIPS (ASSORTED COLOURS): Poppy found them in the bin (Not relevant.)

EMPTY JUICE CARTON: POPPY!

VERDICT: We still don't know what Diana was sacked for, just that it was very, very bad and that she broke more than one rule. This suggests that Diana's career as a dinner lady is definitely over.

NOTE: We have actually broken a Young Super Sleuth Rule! Or Poppy did. Technically speaking, Saffron Cauliflower's lunchbox isn't actually evidence, which means we've stolen it. The lunchbox must be returned as soon as possible.

STOLEN!

S. cauliflower

5:10PM
MYSTERY HQ, ANALYSING NEW EVIDENCE

By the time we got back
to HQ we didn't look like
Masters of Disguise any
more. Poppy's hairnet
was as wonky as my
Mystery Senses felt
and Violet had lipstick
smeared across her
cheek.

Arthur came running into the garden. At first
I thought the bright green face paint he was
wearing was another attempt to be a runner
bean with us. I was wrong.

"Cool costumes! Have you all got new parts in the play too?" he said. "Miss Twist heard me singing, and guess what? I'm not a potato any more, I'm the PEA!"

annoying

Pea face

Poppy looked horrified. Luckily she's really worried Saffron might have recognised us, so she's managing to focus on trying to decide what we should do about the lunchbox and what we have discovered.

Inside HQ, Violet paced anxiously while Poppy slumped on a beanbag.

"I said we should have closed the case when Mr Douglas told us Diana was sacked!" Violet said. "I don't care about finding out what she did – we are just as guilty as she is for stealing that lunchbox. We have been asking so many questions about Diana, Saffron is bound to guess it was us nosing around her offices."

"I'm sure if we just get it back to her she won't report us," Poppy said. (She didn't look very sure.) "At least we know Diana was sacked for serious misconduct now. That's enough for our case report, isn't it?"

What? Serious misconduct and the worst rule breach Saffron has ever seen? If I've been _this_ wrong about Diana Dumpling, I need to know exactly what she has done, especially because I feel like Saffron must have been talking about Diana's evil twin or something.

Diana's EVIL TWIN!

"We can't give up now!" I said. "There might be a copy of the Dinner Lady Code of Conduct in the school kitchens – we could find out what rule 344 actually is!"

Violet folded her arms, like she was a teacher and totally cross.

"Mariella," she said. "We need to drop this before we get ourselves into any more trouble."

Even though all the evidence is telling me Violet is right, I'm just not ready to accept that I'm a rubbish detective who didn't notice that Diana had some sort of dark side. I'm not giving up on finding out what rule 344 is yet, even if Poppy and Violet have.

But for now we have to focus on the fact that we might have our careers ruined too – by that stolen lunchbox. We've put this anonymous note inside the lunchbox and we're going to leave it somewhere Saffron will find it tomorrow.

SORRY.
massive mistake made.
Just retuning your lunchbox
which we have cleaned to
make up for it going
missing for a short time.
THANKS! x

Thursday 21st May

Lunchbox stealers

7:50AM
MY HOUSE, 22 SYCAMORE AVENUE, KITCHEN TABLE

I hardly slept last night. I kept thinking about what rule 344 of the Dinner Lady Code of Conduct might be and worrying that Saffron had already told Miss Twist we'd stolen her lunchbox.

That's why when Dad came into the kitchen and asked if I'd seen the front page of this morning's Puddleford Gazette, I totally expected to see the headline: LUNCHBOX STOLEN BY FAKE DINNER LADY MYSTERY GIRLS.

It wasn't that, though. But it definitely explains why there are loads of kids off school.

PUDDLEFORD GRIPPED BY DINNER LADY'S FINGER

Puddleford is experiencing an outbreak of the highly contagious Dinner Lady's Finger infection. It is reported that dinner ladies suffering from symptoms, including a rash, flaky skin and itchiness, have not followed Dinner Lady Code of Conduct hygiene guidelines and the infection has spread from kitchens into classrooms.

There are twelve confirmed cases of children suffering from Dinner Lady's Finger. In addition, there are rumours of a similar situation in ten other schools in the local area.

Penny Parkinson, mother of eleven year-old Dinner Lady's Finger victim, Primrose Parkinson, shared her reaction:

"My poor princess is missing out on being a real princess in the school play because of unhygienic dinner ladies. Something must be done!"

Miss Twist, headteacher of Puddleford Primary, was quick to dispel fears that Dinner Lady's Finger could cause pupil absences to rise to the alarming levels seen during the Itch-in-a-Mug food crisis two years ago.

"The dinner ladies responsible for spreading this illness have been sent home and this morning the whole kitchen was deep cleaned by the Ladies Who Lunch Supply Dinner Lady Agency. Saffron Cauliflower and her Ladies Who Lunch have taken over the running of the school kitchens and I can assure you there will be no more cases of Dinner Lady's Finger, only extremely tasty school dinners."

Do you think enough is being done to tackle Dinner Lady's Finger and are your children still going to eat school dinners? We leave you with this word from school dinner supporter, Arthur Mystery.

"It's like our lovely new dinner lady, Mrs Cauliflower, says, school dinners are yum, yum, yummy in my TUMMY!"

Share your views with us on the usual number 0800 PUDDLEFORD.

12:45PM
PUDDLEFORD PRIMARY, BACK DOOR OF SCHOOL KITCHENS

I'm actually pleased Poppy stole Saffron's lunchbox now! If we hadn't had to return it, we never would have found out what rule 344 is. (It's nothing to do with Dinner Lady's Finger either – though after reading that article, Violet thinks we should be careful in case we have caught it too.) I'm still in shock.

Finding the right moment to return the lunchbox wasn't easy. We were stuck in emergency play rehearsals all morning. All other classes have been cancelled so that the stand-ins get as much practice as possible. They need it.

Arthur had to call for help halfway through a song because he was stuck under the mattresses on the Princess's bed. His annoying friend Pippa has been cast as the Princess because her sister, Primrose, the original Princess, is sick. Pippa said she knew all the lines from listening to her sister rehearse, but she obviously doesn't.

pea face   pippa

Finally, after lunch, we managed to sneak from the playground to leave the lunchbox outside the kitchen back door.

As we approached, we heard voices coming through the open window. It was Saffron, talking to Mrs Spooner.

open

Mrs Spooner   Saffron

I quickly pulled Violet and Poppy behind the big kitchen wheelie bin. Being caught red-handed with the lunchbox would be totally embarrassing.

"Don't worry about me," Saffron said. She sounded upset. "I'm just having a bad week. First I had to say goodbye to Miss Dumpling, and now all of those children are ill. I feel bad for Miss Button and her team – Dinner Lady's Finger is a serious condition – but they simply weren't following the Dinner Lady Code of Conduct when they came back to work while still infectious."

hiding →

Being nosy

"If anyone can sort this out, you can," Mrs Spooner said. "I was shocked, though, to hear about Miss Dumpling. Not that I want to pry into your reasons for letting her go."

That was a total lie. It was obvious Mrs Spooner wanted to know why Saffron had sacked Diana as much as I did.

"I probably shouldn't say, but it would be good to talk to someone." Saffron sighed. "You won't believe it when I tell you. Miss Dumpling was planning something completely inappropriate for the Ladies Who Lunch staff party next week."

Poppy and Violet looked at me. Staff party? What was Saffron talking about?

"I'd asked Diana to take care of party bags because I thought she would fill them with fun stuff. What she did made me realise I didn't know her as well as I'd thought," Saffron said.

"I found the bags in the storeroom. She was planning to poke fun at the unfortunate sick dinner ladies by putting pots of joke itching powder in them!"

SHocking!

ITCHY DINNER LADY

PARTY

"No!" Mrs Spooner said in disbelief.

"That's what I thought," said Saffron. "Laughing at such a serious issue goes against rule 344 in the Dinner Lady Code of Conduct: Dinner Ladies should take a professional and serious approach to hygiene at all times."

"Oh my! That's such an important rule – what was she thinking?" Mrs Spooner said.

"I told Diana it wasn't funny," Saffron continued, "but she had a huge tantrum and threw one of the party bags at me. Throwing things at other dinner ladies broke yet another rule – rule 225, to be precise. I had no choice but to sack her on the spot."

"I don't blame you!" said Mrs Spooner.

"I can't let things like that slip," said Saffron. "Imagine if the papers got hold of the story? Nobody would hire Ladies Who Lunch ever again."

Mrs Spooner and Saffron moved away from the window and we couldn't hear them any more.

Poppy and Violet gawped at me. I knew what they were thinking. Bad taste party bags and tantrums? NO WAY!

I should be happy that we can
finish our final case report,
but I'm not. I can't believe
Diana isn't the person I
thought she was. And I
am totally annoyed with
myself for wanting to
believe she could never have
messed up, even though the Young
Super Sleuth's Handbook said not to let liking
somebody get in the way of the facts.

my mystery senses Bin

What was I thinking? I can never trust my
Mystery Senses again.

I feel guilty too. The last thing Saffron needs on
top of Dinner Lady's Finger and Diana's party
bag drama is us stealing her things. We left
Saffron's lunchbox by the back door. I hope
she finds it.

Poppy says I have to focus on our performance. I suppose there's nothing else to do. BORING!

Friday 22nd May

I have hung up my detective hat. Because I'm rubbish.

7:20AM
BOTTOM OF THE STAIRS, MY HOUSE

I think I've just found something mysterious, but I'm not totally sure. (Mostly because my Mystery Senses have been so wrong this week that I don't know whether to listen to them or not.)

I was first up this morning and I found Watson (amazing pet cat and sidekick) in the kitchen licking something disgusting and slimy.

Watson

A trail of goo led away across the floor to the washing machine, where the bag with the stinky school dinner Mystery Kit in still sat. (Mum was moaning last night she's been too busy to do washing and that it's Dad's turn.)

I quickly deduced that Watson had ripped open the evidence bags of soggy school dinner-covered rubbish and spread them everywhere.

YUCK! I already felt like a rubbish detective, so I didn't need to find out the Mystery Kit might now always smell a bit like school dinners to remind me of how I'd got Diana Dumpling so totally wrong.

Eau de Diana Dumpling

I realised I should probably take the stuff away from Watson, in case cats can catch Dinner Lady's Finger too. I eventually managed to pull a slimy packet out of his mouth.

I was about to chuck it in the bin and wash my hands when something caught my eye.

Now that Watson had mostly licked it clean, I could see what the packet was – a sachet of Monster Mash flavoured Meal-in-a-Mug, the banned instant meal range that Arthur is allergic to.

Exhibit A: Meal-in-a-Mug

MEAL & PUD in-a MUG

MONSTER MASH!

At first I thought Watson had somehow found the multipack at the back of the kitchen cupboard, but I've just looked and the box is still unopened.

That means this packet must be from the school kitchen bin. WHAT was it doing in there? It definitely doesn't seem like the sort of thing you'd want near school dinners, not when it causes terrible allergic reactions.

It was disgusting, but I knew I should check the other bags of gloopy rubbish to see if Poppy had accidentally collected anything else interesting. I rinsed the contents of the bags under the kitchen tap ... and found another strange packet. It was Jelly Jitter Critter flavoured Pud-in-a-Mug!

WEIRD ALERT!

Everyone knows not to eat Meal and Pud-in-a-Mugs after the Itch-in-a-Mug scandal. Since it's turned out Diana didn't care much about the rules, maybe eating banned soup is just the sort of crazy thing she'd do. But I still don't understand why she, or anyone else would want to – not when it makes you ill.

Poppy and Violet will probably tell me I should drop it, but what sort of detective would ignore the discovery of TWO illegal soup packets of what has been classed a hazardous foodstuff in their school kitchen bin?

toxic soup!

Scenery

PEAS

9:45AM
PUDDLEFORD PRIMARY HALL, FINAL PLAY RUN-THROUGH

Being a detective is so frustrating sometimes – especially when you start seeing mysteries where there are none.

There were so many announcements this morning about everyone being on best behaviour when parents arrive to watch the play that the first chance I got to talk to Poppy and Violet was when Miss Crumble told our class to wait on the benches next to the stage.

Scrambled mystery senses

Violet was stressed
because Poppy has
a lumpy rash on her
arms. Mystery Girl with
a potential case of Dinner
Lady's Finger alert!

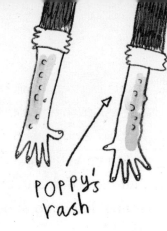

Poppy's
rash

"I'm fine – I'm sure it's not Dinner
Lady's Finger," Poppy said. "My Aunty
Pat got a rash because she was stressed and it's
been really stressful getting ready for the play
and investigating Diana."

"You've caught it from all that stuff you touched
in the bin on Monday!" Violet said, ignoring
Poppy. "I bet we've all got it now! You should
tell a teacher." She was madly patting her arms
and legs.

"About that rubbish Poppy collected," I said. "I
think there was something interesting in there."

I told them about the Meal-in-a-Mug packets.

"I love mystery too, Mariella, but there are loads of reasons the soup packets could have been in the bin," Poppy said. "A dinner lady probably had them at home at the back of a cupboard, like your mum did, and brought them in for lunch without knowing about them being banned."

Maybe. Is it possible not everyone knows about the Itch-in-a-Mug crisis like I thought they did? I suppose somebody who missed all the news stories might not.

"Mariella, those packets need to go back in the bin – they must be covered in germs!" Violet said. "You probably have Dinner Lady's Finger now too!"

Eurgh, I hope not. But I'm starting to think the lack of a real mystery situation has sent me a bit crazy.

me, crazy and itchy

LOOKING AFTER YOUR MYSTERY SENSES

You may love mystery, but constant detective work can mess up your Mystery Senses, causing you to miss clues and make dodgy deductions. Be constantly vigilant for signs of muddled Mystery Senses and take steps to avoid mystery meltdown.

Exhibit A: Young Detective Suffering From Muddled Mystery Senses

Too afraid to talk to angry clients

Exhausted from late night deductions

Disorganised evidence filing system

Working alone due to arguing with fellow mystery solvers while stressed.

Huge pile of unsolved mysteries

Exhibit B: Young Detective with Mind-boggling Mystery Senses

Relaxed and alert

Organised filing system

Appropriate case-load

Supportive mystery sidekick

Ways to Refresh Your Mystery Senses:

Take a long bubble bath

Read a mystery story

Do yoga

TOP TIP While it's important to take regular breaks it's not advisable to nap in a chase situation in case your suspect gets away.

10:45AM
SCHOOL HALL, PLAY REHEARSALS
INTERRUPTED

Unbelievable stuff just happened!

Arthur was on stage, his green face peeking out from underneath a stack of mattresses and duvets. Miss Twist was telling him – again – that he wasn't supposed to be squeaking at this point in the play.

E*eeeeee.*E*eeee.*

EEEEEEE!

Suddenly, Arthur rolled out from under the
mattress and started wriggling around and
banging into the legs of Princess and the Queen.
I thought he was channelling his inner pea or
something but it was a bit odd, even for Arthur.

"Get up this instant!" Miss Twist said.

"I can't! I'm itchy! It's itching all over," Arthur
squealed.

Everyone on stage backed away. Roberta Poppet
shouted that he had Dinner Lady's Finger.

"Right, I don't care what Poppy says. She is
infected, and so is Arthur, which means that you
probably definitely are too," Violet said. "You
need to put those packets in the bin. NOW!"

111

"Is that what's going to happen to me?" Poppy said. "This is all Diana's fault! If she hadn't got herself sacked, I wouldn't have had to look through the kitchen bin!"

Even though I didn't feel itchy, I agreed to throw the packets away before Violet had a breakdown.

Arthur was out of his pea costume now and couldn't stop wriggling around and itching himself like a crazy person. The teachers were trying to get him out of the hall without touching him. He was being totally dramatic. It was exactly like when he got itchy from eating the Monster Mash Meal-in-a-Mug.

itch itch itch

Hmmm.

Hmmm.

But this was Dinner Lady's Finger ... wasn't it? It couldn't have anything to do with the sachets of Meal-in-a-Mug we found in the kitchens ... or could it?

HANG ON.

The *Puddleford Gazette* article said that the infected dinner ladies were sent home and that Ladies Who Lunch deep cleaned our kitchen yesterday, so there shouldn't be any new cases of Dinner Lady's Finger. But Arthur is itchy and we know for sure Meal and Pud-in-a-Mug have been in the kitchens!

DEEP Clean?

Flaky skin

The Young Super Sleuth's Handbook says that even though coincidences can happen, any slightly suspicious coincidence should be investigated further – just in case.

"I know you'll tell me I'm crazy, but don't you think it's a bit weird that Dinner Lady's Finger has similar symptoms to the itchy reaction caused by the Meal and Pud-in-a-Mug crisis?" I said.

Violet looked unimpressed. Poppy raised her eyebrows.

"But, Mariella, in case you haven't noticed, we haven't been served soups and puddings in mugs for school dinners," Violet said.

"Meal and Pud-in-a-Mugs have definitely been in the kitchens, though, and now Arthur, who is allergic to Meal and Pud-in-a-Mugs, is itchy, even though the kitchen is supposed to have been deep cleaned," I said. "I think we should do another search of the kitchen."

toxic

Operation Search for Scratchy Soup and Probe for Prohibited Puddings

NOTE: The following events happened so quickly I didn't get chance to report back at the time.

CAUTION: Do not read further if you are of a nervous disposition. The tension and disbelief will be too much for you to handle.

11:45AM
SCHOOL KITCHENS, NO DINNER LADIES IN SIGHT

Parents had started to arrive for the play and were busy gossiping about the Dinner Lady's Finger situation. Mum and Dad waved as they walked back in the hall from visiting Arthur in the sick bay.

Dad

mum

I was beginning to think getting into the kitchen would be impossible, until I saw the dinner ladies had finished carrying trays of fancy-looking school dinner canapés to the back of the hall and were taking their seats on the back row.

Fancy

SCHOOL DINNER CANAPÉS

If they were going to be watching the play, that meant the kitchens would be empty. Perfect! We had fifteen minutes before the performance started.

I told Violet and Poppy to follow me and act casual. Nobody noticed us disappear through the swinging door.

The kitchen was messier than it had been on Monday. There were bowls by the sink and spilled ingredients. In the serving area were silver tubs of school dinners, ready to be served when the parents were gone.

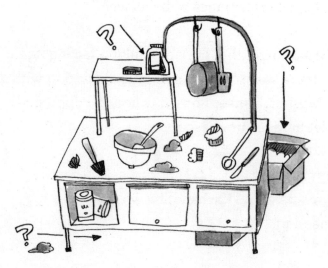

Violet looked under the counters and I checked the pockets of the dinner ladies' coats hanging by the door. Poppy examined the plates and cups neatly stacked on metal shelves. There wasn't a Meal or Pud-in-a-Mug packet or granule in sight.

The chatter in the hall fell silent and music began. The play had started.

"I knew we wouldn't find anything. Let's just go," said Violet.

"Yeah. We can't miss our big entrance," Poppy said. "This week has been a mystery flop – I don't want our performance to be as well."

I started to get that horrible sinking feeling again that there was something drastically wrong with my Mystery Senses and I'd dragged Poppy and Violet here for no reason.

"Hang on – what's this?" Poppy said from the other side of the kitchen. She was pointing to something.

I moved closer. On the white tiled floor was a trail of red powder with small, uncooked wiggly pasta shapes in it. It looked very like the sort of stuff you find in packets of instant soup.

I grabbed the box of Meal and Pud-in-a-Mugs that I'd brought from home, pulled out the Tingling Tomato Taste Explosion flavour and ripped it open.

"What are you doing? Don't open that – it's a hazardous food stuff!" Violet said.

I poured a bit of the packet onto the floor, next to the powder Poppy had discovered. It was the same colour and had the exact same tiny wiggly pieces of pasta in it.

"It's Meal-in-a-Mug!" Poppy said.

THE SAME!

12:02PM
SCHOOL KITCHENS, MAKING AN
UNBELIEVABLE DISCOVERY

On closer inspection, I could see
that the trail of soup granules
stretched towards the corner
of the kitchen, under the door
of the storeroom.

I ran to the door and pulled it
open. The shelves were stacked
with giant tins of beans and
packets of burger buns, but
there was no sign of any
Meal or Pud-in-a-Mug
packets.

Then I spotted something else – loads of silver containers with little handwritten labels. The scrawly handwriting said they were flavouring mixes for school dinner dishes – Pirate Pasta Bake, Cheesy Chomp, and others we hadn't tried yet.

CHEESY CHOMP

mango melt

Pirate Pasta

Princess Pie

Flavouring mixes

"The dinner ladies must use these to make all the tasty sauces," Violet said.

I unscrewed the lid on the jar labelled as Pirate Pasta Bake Flavour mix. What I found was totally unbelievable.

The jar was filled with orange powder and skull-and-cross-bone shaped pasta. My heart started to race.

Pirate Pasta

"It's Meal-in-a-Mug! It's been tipped out into this container!" I said.

"It can't be," said Violet. "It says it's the flavouring for the Pirate Pasta Bake. We ate that skull pasta the other day. It was mixed in with that gooey sauce and vegetables but I remember those pasta shapes."

Violet was right. Of course this wasn't Meal-in-a-Mug.

Unless...

multipack box

"What if the Pirate Pasta Bake was made using Meal-in-a-Mug?" I said. "Pass me the multipack box!"

"Mariella, are you OK?" Violet said. "I think the stress of this case is getting to you. School dinners couldn't possibly be made with Meal-in-a-Mug! That would be dangerous."

I flicked through the different flavours, Jelly Jitter Critter Pudding, Monster Mash Soup, Noodle Doodle Dinner. I pulled out a packet of the Witches' Brew Stew Flavour. Ripping it open, I poured the contents out on to the floor, next to the Pirate Pasta Bake sauce mix.

They were exactly the same colour, with exactly the same pasta shapes in them! They just had a different name and the one we'd eaten for school dinners hadn't been served in a mug. It was the same pasta but in a thick sauce with vegetables and cheese on top.

Violet gasped and Poppy clapped her hand over her mouth.

"We should check the other sauce mixes!" I said.

Violet pulled the lid off the
Princess Pie mix.

"It's pink powder with frog
sweets in! Oh no. They're
Pud-in-a-Mug granules,
aren't they?" she said.

Poppy ripped open the Jelly Jitter
Critter Pud-in-a-Mug sachet and poured
some out. It was the same as the stuff in the jar
Violet was holding. The only difference
was that the pudding
we'd eaten on Monday
had had sweets added
and been made into a
massive jelly.

Princess
Pie

We opened more sauce
mix jars. They were all filled with different
coloured powders that we matched to the Meal
and Pud-in-a-Mug granules! But they had been
served with extra ingredients mixed in, so of
course nobody would guess they were eating
banned soup and puddings.

This was CRAZY. All our school meals were being made with banned hazardous Meals and Puds-in-a-Mug!

"This is the reason I've got a rash. I've been eating banned food!" Poppy said, horrified. "You were right about Arthur, and I bet those other kids who are supposed to have caught Dinner Lady's Finger are all just having allergic reactions to school dinners too. Actually, is that what has been wrong with the dinner ladies as well?"

Poppy had a point. I was sure the Young Super Sleuth's Handbook would say it was no coincidence that so many itchy people were in one place.

"If itchy dinner ladies aren't connected to Meal and Pud-in-a-Mug I'd be very surprised," I said. "But when the Big G and her team first went home sick they were just serving normal school dinners, so how did they get itchy?"

"I don't know, but I feel itchy, I feel sick, I feel … argh!" Violet said.

My head spun with unanswered questions about Dinner Lady's Finger, banned soups and puddings – but mostly with thoughts of Diana Dumpling.

We knew she'd done some weird stuff and that she thought itchy dinner ladies were funny. Was she the one behind this? Was this the real, truly terrible reason Saffron sacked her? And if that was true, WHY were Meal and Pud-in-a-Mugs still being served?

DERANGED

DINNER LADY

EXPOSING A SCANDAL

A scandal is when something shocking and unexpected is revealed about a person or organisation. Knowing what to do in order to expose the truth is essential.

Levels of Scandal:

SKELETON IN THE CLOSET: When an upstanding person has been leading a double life and is not who they say they are.

OUTRAGEOUS: When somebody who previously seemed trustworthy, like a teacher, does something wild. Like framing a pupil for a bad deed.

JAW-DROPPINGLY SHOCKING: When a large number of people are completely fooled by an individual who may have run off with their life savings, or persuaded them to buy fake antique teapots.

Librarian · Criminal

It was him

Fake

DON'T waste time saying things like, "This can't be true. She was such a wonderful babysitter!"

Shocked

Photogenic

DO ensure you have a flattering photograph of yourself for newspapers to use when they report on how you uncovered the scandal.

SCANDAL ALERT!

DON'T get distracted by thoughts of how brilliant exposing this scandal will be for your career. (Your suspect might escape.)

I'll be famous!

DO call the authorities or make a very loud announcement sharing what you have discovered before suspects can hide evidence or leave the country.

WARNING

Discovering a surprising secret about somebody, like that your teacher's middle name is Efflebottom, doesn't necessarily mean you have uncovered a scandal. In this instance revealing the truth may cause unnecessary embarrassment.

I'm so ashamed!

12:10PM
KITCHEN STOREROOM, IN SHOCK

There was a loud gasp from the audience in the hall, as if they knew the terrible thing we had discovered.

"I can't believe Diana was so excited about us swapping to hot dinners," Violet said. "She must have known this is what we would have been eating. She invented every single recipe on Saffron's menu! How could Saffron not know about this? Unless she did and she is covering up to avoid a huge scandal?"

Adding deliberate poisoning to Diana's list of misconducts and realising there was the possibility that Saffron may have continued to serve toxic food (even though she'd sacked Diana for serving it) was a lot to process. Even for my genius detective brain.

"Maybe Diana fooled Saffron like she fooled us. But if Saffron knows about what is really in these jars and she still let everyone eat it, well, that makes her just as bad as Diana," I said.

"We've got to tell Miss Twist what we've uncovered! " Poppy said, standing up.

I was about to say that yes, we totally needed to expose the truth – and to stop anyone eating what must be dangerous Meal and Pud-in-a-Mug school dinner canapés – when I spotted an official-looking notebook right at the back of the shelf.

"Look at this!" I said. "Maybe it's Diana's secret recipe book of toxic ingredients."

But it wasn't. On the front was written 'Ladies Who Lunch Weekly Planner, property of Saffron Cauliflower'.

I didn't move for a second because I was busy having a Moment of Suspicion. The planner had been right at the back of the shelf. Had it accidentally been pushed there when the sauce mix containers were used? Or had it had been deliberately hidden so nobody would see it?

"Mariella, we haven't got time to sit around, we've got to warn people," Violet said. "Come on!"

It's a good job I ignored Violet because as I flicked through the pages I realised that this was most certainly something Saffron Cauliflower did not want anyone to see.

TURN OVER
FOR SHOCKING
STUFF!

LADIES WHO LUNCH

MONDAY

1. Order fancy plates for school dinner canapés.

2. SACK Dumpling features — she knows too much.

TUESDAY

1. Sprinkle Tingling Tomato granules in annoying dinner ladies' uniforms

2. Order cleaning products. We'll need them when Glenda Button and her team call in to say Dinner Lady's finger is back! As if!

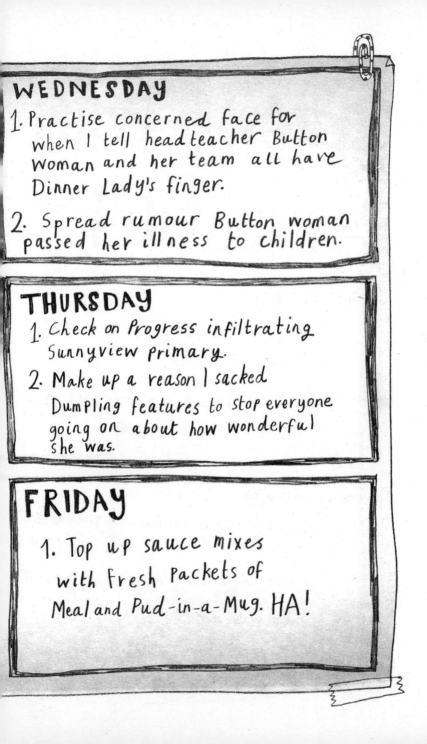

WEDNESDAY

1. Practise concerned face for when I tell headteacher Button Woman and her team all have Dinner Lady's finger.

2. Spread rumour Button woman passed her illness to children.

THURSDAY

1. Check on progress infiltrating Sunnyview primary.

2. Make up a reason I sacked Dumpling features to stop everyone going on about how wonderful she was.

FRIDAY

1. Top up sauce mixes with fresh packets of Meal and Pud-in-a-Mug. HA!

12:15PM
STILL IN THE KITCHEN STOREROOM, TRYING NOT TO PASS OUT

"NO WAY!" Poppy said, grabbing the planner.

"What? Wait. No!" Violet said.

I was grinning. This was the most amazingly useful bit of evidence we'd found all week. It revealed that Saffron Cauliflower was the dastardly dinner lady – not Diana! My Mystery Senses hadn't been short-circuiting. Diana Dumpling, star dinner lady, really does exist!

The REAL dastardly dinner lady

The happy I-told-you-so feeling didn't last long, though. Not when I thought about how Saffron had fooled us for so long. I could have kicked myself for not being more suspicious of her, especially when she refused to talk to us and we knew she'd lied about the dishwasher.

itch!
itch!
itch!
itch!

"What sort of crazy food is this?" Poppy said. "It makes you itchy when you touch it? The poor Big G!"

"Let me get this straight – nobody has Dinner Lady's Finger?" Violet said. "Saffron just made it look like they did so she could take over school kitchens? But why is she feeding us banned soups and puddings?"

I wasn't sure, but what I did know was that with the high levels of unexpected twists and turns in this case, it was probably for a reason we would never guess in a million years.

"We still need to figure that out, but at least now we know Diana was sacked unfairly," I said. "Maybe Diana knew about Meal and Pud-in-a-Mugs and was trying to stop Saffron? That must be what she meant by 'things are not what they seem' on her recipe!"

"I feel terrible for believing the story about the party bags," Violet said.

"Never mind that," said Poppy. "Look at this!"

She was pointing to something on the back of the Jelly Jitter Critter pack.

"Yum Yum in my tum," was written on the back of every flavour, next to the smiling face of TV chef, Arabella Flump, who had been banned from ever cooking for anyone again after the Itch-in-a-Mug crisis.

"That's exactly what Saffron says, all the time!" I said. "Wow, she must have been pretty sure no one would ever guess what she was up to!"

"Hang on. Is Saffron related to that woman on the back of the packet or something?" Poppy said.

I looked at the packet again. Saffron wears different glasses to the TV chef Arabella Flump, and has a hairnet. But I could see what Poppy meant – they did look similar, sort of.

(SAFFRON CAULIFLOWER

ARABELLA FLUMP)

"Sorry to interrupt you, but what exactly are you doing in my storeroom?" a voice behind us said.

nasty cauliflower

12:20PM
SCHOOL KITCHENS,
FACE TO FACE WITH A CUNNING CAULIFLOWER

It was Dastardly Dinner Lady Saffron Cauliflower!
She was smiling, and the weird thing was that
she didn't look even a bit angry we'd uncovered
her shocking secret.

I was about to say the
sort of thing a genius
detective would say,
like "You can't pull
the dirty dishcloth
over our eyes any
more, Saffron!" But
Poppy beat me to it.

Argh! Cauliflower

"You! You gave me a rash!" she screamed. "You've made loads of people ill! Well, we know about the special secret ingredient you've been putting in our school dinners!"

Saffron carried on smiling, but her eyes flashed to the mess of granules and Meal and Pud-in-a-Mug packets on the floor.

"Yeah, and I know secret ingredients are meant to stay secret, but there's no way we are keeping this quiet, Cauliflower," I said.

It felt really good calling Saffron by her last name. I hoped that would annoy her and make her finally drop the stupid Fake-Delightful-Dinner-Lady act.

"Pick a Pea, Pick me! I never liked the garden anyway!"

The sound of singing came from the hall. It was almost time for us to be on stage.

PEAS

Poppy looked more
furious than ever. I didn't
blame her. Not only did
she have a rash, but
Saffron was messing up
our big entrance in the play.

POPPY
fuming

"I'm sure I don't know what you
mean," Saffron said. "Now, I think we need to
tidy up this mess you've made. Don't you?"

Poppy and Violet looked at me, unsure what to
do. Thinking quickly, I used a technique from the
Young Super Sleuth's Handbook called Creating a
Distraction.

"Look, Miss Twist is here. She can help you tidy
the cupboard," I said, gesturing towards the
kitchen door.

It worked. Saffron spun around.

"RUN!" I shouted.

12:25PM
SCHOOL HALL, CARRYING HAZARDOUS
FOODSTUFFS

BANG!

Poppy pushed open the kitchen door so hard it
bounced off the wall. All the parents turned to
see three runner beans racing out of the kitchen.
Glancing behind, I saw Saffron had stopped in
the doorway. She seemed undecided whether to
chase us or attempt to dispose of the evidence in
the kitchen.

running
beans →

Mum took a photo and gave me the thumbs-up. Some of the other parents smiled too. Arthur's friend, Pippa, stopped dancing with the empty pea costume

Empty

on stage and stared at us. Miss Twist was pointing madly at the benches where we were supposed to be sitting.

The Young Super Sleuth's Handbook says to always carefully prepare a speech and to appear calm before making public announcements. So escaping from a deranged dinner lady while dressed as a runner bean wasn't the most ideal way to reveal what we'd uncovered, but we couldn't wait and risk Saffron moving the evidence.

"Saffron Cauliflower has been feeding us all banned Meal and Pud-in-a-Mugs – the stuff there was a big scandal about two years ago that made everyone itchy!" I shouted.

It was supposed to come out in my serious detective voice, but instead it came out in sort of a rush and very high-pitched.

To my surprise, nobody looked as horrified as I thought they would. They just seemed confused and as if they thought I should sit down if I wasn't going to sing a nice song. Mum and Dad were both blushing bright red.

Embarrassed

"Mariella Mystery, I am shocked," Miss Twist said finally.

Great! I thought. This is a massive school dinner scandal, so you should be. But she wasn't talking about the school dinners.

Not happy

"I expect this sort of show-off stunt from Poppy Holmes, but not you and Violet Maple," she continued.

Parents were looking away now, raising their eyebrows and muttering. Mum was pretending she didn't know me.

"Don't be too hard on them," Saffron said. "I think our super school dinners must have given them super-powered imaginations. Of course, performing will only make them more overexcited. The best thing would be for them to wait with me in the kitchen until the play finishes."

Super-powered imaginations? What a load of rubbish. There was no way we were going with her.

itchy brain

"We've got evidence! These containers are filled with banned Meal and Pud-in-a-Mugs!" I said. "And if you look in the kitchen, the storeroom has even more!"

evidence

Whispers rippled through the hall. Did anyone believe us?

"Enough!" Miss Twist shouted.

"Yes, come on, girls, don't spoil the play any more than you already have," Saffron said.

Violet hid behind my shoulder. Poppy backed away. The Young Super Sleuth's Handbook says that if nobody believes your accusations, you may as well have not bothered solving the mystery because your reputation will be ruined forever. This was a disaster.

Then ...

BANG!

The door leading from the school reception was flung open.

Standing in the doorway, red-faced and windswept, was the Disappearing Dinner Lady – Diana Dumpling!

Diana!
(still wearing her hairnet.)

Pea decorations

12:30PM
SCHOOL HALL, WITH A DISAPPEARING DINNER LADY

Diana's eyes immediately flashed to the silver containers of Meal and Pud-in-a-Mugs that me, Poppy and Violet were holding. I could tell she knew we had figured it out.

"What the Mystery Girls have said about the Cauliflower woman is true!" Diana said to the shocked faces in the hall.

This was the Diana Dumpling we knew, with some added Mystery Girl attitude! Where had this come from? And why now?

"Saffron Cauliflower has tricked you into thinking her school dinners are the best around, just like she tricked me into believing I was creating recipes that used vitamin-enriched powdered vegetables!" Diana shouted. "I've been too afraid to speak out because she threatened to tell everyone it was all my idea ... until I realised I'd feel guilty forever if I let this carry on. I'm too late to stop innocent children eating dangerous food, but I can stop parents falling ill from eating those canapés!"

Go, Diana!

"You all deserve to know the truth about how dinner ladies in this school – and in others – have been made to look as if they have an unhygienic illness when they haven't," Diana continued. She fixed her eyes on Saffron. "None of those dinner ladies deserved to have toxic soup granules put in their uniforms!"

Parents in the audience looked really confused now. The dinner ladies sitting in the back row were staring at Diana in disbelief. Saffron had turned a funny shade of purple.

PURPLE

"Do not listen to this woman," Saffron said. "I had to sack her for serious misconduct. She was making fun of the poor Dinner Lady's Finger victims and she threw a party bag at me!"

"FIBBER!" Poppy screamed, grabbing Saffron's planner off me and waving it in the air. "That's a total lie and we've got proof!"

Miss Twist was gazing from Saffron to Diana.

"Saffron Cauliflower is not the dinner lady you think she is, and I can prove it," Diana said, folding her arms.

"Can't I, Saffron? Or should I say ARABELLA FLUMP, disgraced TV chef and maker of the only instant meal and pudding range ever to be banned because it can cause horrible symptoms, like uncontrollable itching!" Diana continued. "At least her terrible mug creation was mixed in with other ingredients to disguise it, or the symptoms being suffered by children would be just as bad, if not worse, than during the Itch-in-a-Mug scandal."

WHAT? Saffron was Arabella Flump? Of course!

ARABELLA
FLUMP-i-flower!!!

The whole hall gasped so loudly I felt like air should be rushing past my face. They believed Diana! (Maybe me breaking the news to them dressed as a runner bean had made it hard for them to take seriously.)

"I am Saffron Cauliflower. I make delicious school dinners!" Arabella shouted.

She looked desperately at the cast of *The Princess and the Pea* gathered around the stage.

"Don't I, children? What do we always say about school dinners?" she beamed and rubbed her tummy. "Yum yum in my tum!"

What? She'd totally given the game away herself now! HA!

yum yum in my TUM!

"Funny you should say that, Saffron Whoever-you-are," I said. "That's exactly what you wrote on the back of Meal and Pud-in-a-Mug packets."

Violet and Poppy held up the evidence so everyone could see. Miss Twist grabbed one of the packets and stared at it.

Mrs Spooner leaped from her seat and yanked off Saffron's hairnet. Masses of blonde curly hair tumbled out. Saffron did not look like Saffron any more – she looked like Arabella Flump. (Because that's who she really was.)

"She tricked us! She's tricked us all!" Mrs Spooner shouted.

12:35PM
SCHOOL HALL WITH FAKE DINNER LADY,
ARABELLA FLUMP

Everyone was now looking at Saffron (or
Arabella) in disgust.

"Mrs Cauliflower, I mean Flump. Or whoever
you are, get out of my school – immediately!"
Miss Twist said angrily. "The Ministry of School
Dinners will be hearing about what you've done!"

Mr Muffet, the Year Two teacher, and Miss
Crumble got up and started to escort Arabella
out of the hall.

HORRIFIED!

"I don't know what you're making such a fuss about. Your kids have been eating my Meal and Pud-in-a-Mugs for weeks thinking they're delicious, because they are!" Arabella shrieked. "Only a few of them got itchy! And the dinner ladies I got rid of were rubbish anyway!"

Mr Muffet pulled on Arabella's apron. Miss Crumble pushed her towards the door.

"How you ever called yourself a children's chef, I do not know!" Diana said, as Miss Crumble and Mr Muffet give Arabella a final shove out of the hall.

Wow. Diana had totally stood up for herself!
She is the best expert witness we've ever had
in an investigation! (It took her a while to come
forward, but after what she's been through, I
think we can let her off.)

"A bit of itching never hurt anyone!" Saffron
screamed, her voice fading away down the
corridor. "Your kids would have got used to the
food **EVENTUAAAALLLLY**!"

There was a stunned silence.

Then Arthur's friend Pippa's mum started to clap.
"Hooray for the Mystery Girls!" she yelled.
"Without them whole families could have ended
up itchy! And hooray! My
daughter Primrose isn't
suffering from a highly
contagious disease
she is just having an
allergic reaction!"

So happy
she could
cry

There were whoops and cheers from the other parents, and the Ladies Who Lunch dinner ladies and everyone on stage. And lots of clapping. Mum was proudly telling the woman next to her I was her daughter.

"You don't need to thank us," I said, as the noise quietened down. "It was all in a day's work for the Mystery Girls, and a bit of assistance from a key witness star dinner lady, Diana Dumpling always helps."

There was loads more clapping and Diana blushed. Poppy and Violet hugged me and started jumping up and down, which felt amazing, but made it a bit hard to say my closing line. (It's always good to say something interesting when you have solved a case so that people think you are even cleverer than they already do.)

"Now may I suggest, the show must go on!" I said. (Really I wanted to stay and listen to everyone tell us how great we are, but the Young Super Sleuth's Handbook says that detectives shouldn't soak up the praise too much or everyone will think you are just in it for the glory.)

"I would also like to issue one last piece of Mystery Girl advice. Do not eat those canapés – you might get very itchy indeed," I said.

"Definitely," called Diana, "I'll make you some fresh ones, without any suspicious ingredients at all!"

Everyone clapped and whooped again. I probably should have stopped them, but a little more celebration never hurt anyone!

**11:00AM
MYSTERY GIRL HQ, EATING LEFT OVER
MONDAY MUNCHIE PUDDING. YUM!**

I'm still grinning just as much as I was yesterday
because we managed to get the full story about
Diana Dumpling and we totally exposed the
biggest school dinner scandal EVER.

When Arthur was released from the nurse's office, he tried to hug me while everyone was looking. I did not look cool and professional with an itchy, squeaking pea hanging off me. But we'd proved that Arthur was having an allergic reaction, and wasn't actually contagious, so he was allowed to come back and play the part of the Pea.

I'm glad I don't seem to be allergic to Meal and Pud-in-a-Mugs because the itchiness looks really awful. Poppy's rash has almost gone now, but she had a lucky escape. Meal and Pud-in-a-Mugs affect people in different ways depending on how bad their allergy to it is.

Poppy was lucky just to have a rash, but if she had eaten more Meal and Pud-in-a-Mugs her symptoms may have got worse and she would eventually have ended up in the same state as Arthur or some of the kids who were off school.

vomit

If Saffron hadn't disguised Meal and Pud-in-a-Mugs as school dinners, with added ingredients like vegetables, pasty crusts and cheesy toppings, the Mystery Girls would have figured the whole thing out far sooner.

mild allergy

We got another really big cheer when we made our entrance as runner beans. I'm not sure true Masters of Disguise would do this, but we did come out of character and make a little bow to the audience.

Best BEANS ever

Diana organised the other dinner ladies to whip up some tasty new school dinner canapés. She made a massive batch of Monday Munchie Madness Chocolate Pudding too, even though it was a Friday, and it totally does taste like a cloud of chocolate melting in your mouth.

PEa garnish

yummy

I got a bit sad when the play was over and lunch had finished, because now that we knew the Big G and the other dinner ladies didn't really have Dinner Lady's Finger, it meant that Diana Dumpling wouldn't work in our school any more.

But we got some amazing news when Miss Twist announced that she wanted to offer Diana a job as Dinner-Lady-in-Charge of Recipe Development!

Diana looked as if she might cry with happiness when it happened – and she said yes, as long as Miss Button (The Big G) agreed to it when she returned.

DElighted

The police are investigating Arabella Flump in partnership with the Ministry of School Dinners. They have been speaking to the dinner ladies who had Meal and Pud-in-a-Mugs used against them and plan to charge Arabella with Food Crimes of an Itchy Nature.

They've never seen a case like it, and Arabella might even go to prison. (Apparently she has already been told she won't be allowed anywhere near the kitchens there.)

The whole of Puddleford knows about the case of the Disappearing Dinner Lady. Wherever we go, we get clapped! I haven't had a chance to write up the whole story, until now.

CASE REPORT: THE DISAPPEARING DINNER LADY

Diana Dumpling didn't actually disappear. She went into hiding after being sacked from the Ladies Who Lunch supply dinner lady agency because she had discovered the terrible truth about the sinister ingredient being used to make school dinners.

Saffron Cauliflower was actually Arabella Flump, the celebrity children's chef, whose reputation was ruined after a scandal surrounding her range of instant Meal and Pud-in-a-Mugs, which caused severe itching and vomiting in children.

Arabella
"itch-in-a mug" →
FLUMP

Convinced the itching scandal was a lot of fuss about nothing, and with a celebrity lifestyle to fund, Arabella combined her knowledge of cookery and her huge supply of banned Meal and Pud-in-a-Mugs to terrible effect. She decided to disguise and sell the sachets to a new, unsuspecting market - school dinners.

Arabella set up Ladies Who Lunch and became Saffron Cauliflower. She tipped the Meal-in-a-Mugs into large containers and re-labelled them as food flavouring mixes. None of the dinner ladies she employed guessed that they were actually using banned meals and puddings in their school dinners.

Arabella's mansion

Flavouring mixes

One afternoon, Diana walked into Arabella's office without knocking and discovered her without her hairnet on, tipping Meal-in-a-Mug sachets into jars. Everyone knew Arabella Flump had been banned from cooking for people ever again, and using ingredients that would make children ill went against all Diana's Dinner Lady Training.

Arabella told Diana that if she breathed a word, she would make everyone believe that Diana had known about the ingredients when she developed her school dinner recipes. Terrified that her lifelong dream of a career as a dinner lady would be ruined, Diana continued to work for Arabella for a number of weeks after her shocking discovery.

Arabella was able to infiltrate Puddleford Primary as well as ten other primary schools by making existing dinner ladies believe they were suffering from Dinner Lady's Finger. Dinner Lady's Finger is a real illness, but it wasn't what was making the dinner ladies sick. Arabella had sent them new uniforms contaminated with undiluted Meal-in-a-Mug granules.

hairnets

The packages were falsely marked as being from the Official Ministry of School Dinners Uniform Department. Because they weren't diluted with water or anything else at all, the granules acted as powerful itching powder, causing a bad rash within minutes of coming into contact with skin.

ministry of school dinners

Puddleford Primary kitchens

After consuming school dinners containing Meal and Pud-in-a-Mugs, some children who were especially sensitive to the mixtures' banned contents began to fall ill with severe itching. Nobody suspected in a million years they were eating Meal and Pud-in-a-Mugs, so the finger of blame was pointed at Dinner Lady's Finger and unhygienic dinner ladies.

itchy finger of blame

Arabella was sure that children would become less itchy once they were used to school dinners, allowing her to make a fortune while getting rid of her stash of Meal and Pud-in-a-Mugs. She thought if she made the existing dinner ladies look bad, she would be able to steal their jobs permanently.

Arabella's school dinner fortune

On Monday, Arabella realised Diana had been making Monday Munchie Madness Pudding without using Pud-in-a-Mug granules. When Diana tried to stand up for herself, Arabella decided she couldn't be trusted and sacked her.

As she was being thrown out of the kitchen, Diana screamed. The Mystery Girls heard this and thought it was highly suspicious. What Arabella didn't know was that Diana had been planning to tip us off after school with a note saying 'things are not what they seem'.

Diana had planned to write more but she was forced to leave before she could finish. After she lost her job, she was so upset, worried and confused that she ignored our attempts to contact her.

Diana in bed

Arabella attempted to throw everyone off the scent of what had really happened by making up a terrible story about Diana and bad taste party bags.

Fortunately evidence emerged allowing us to link Ladies Who Lunch to the outbreak of fake Dinner Lady's Finger in dinner ladies and children to their school dinners - two sachets of Meal-in-a-Mug discovered in the kitchen bin.

With so many schools to supply Arabella got sloppy, just like one of her mug-based snacks. Ha!

CASE CLOSED.

NOTE: We are still trying to persuade our head teacher, Miss Twist, that the Mystery Girls should be entitled to a free pass to the front of the queue as reward for our school dinner saving skills. She said we were pushing our luck.

Three beans and a STAR dinner lady!

ACKNOWLEDGEMENTS

I'd like to say a big thank you to the wonderful people who have helped me develop *The Disappearing Dinner Lady* and the rest of Mariella's mysteries. Firstly, a standing ovation for my editor and honorary Mystery Girl, Jenny Glencross, for her wonderful ideas and keen mystery solving mind. A massive *totally* amazing whoop for everyone at Orion for getting behind Mariella and for helping to spread the word of the Mystery Girls far and wide. And lastly a huge round of applause for my husband, Simon, as reward for listening to me talk mystery so much he can be a Mystery Girl too, if he likes.

Kate Pankhurst, May 2015